Hooked by the BBC

A Cuckolding Fantasy

Book 1 in the *Hooked by the BBC Series*

Amber Carden

CHAPTER ONE: Sleepless Nights.......................... 1

CHAPTER TWO: Endless Worries...................... 12

CHAPTER THREE: Unveiling Fantasies........... 24

CHAPTER FOUR: Surrounding Control........... 36

CHAPTER FIVE: Coital Bliss 46

CHAPTER SIX: A New Identity.......................... 55

CHAPTER SEVEN: Mingling Desires 66

CHAPTER ONE:
Sleepless Nights

Mike lay awake in his bed with his wife of fifteen years beside him. He could hear the sound of her breathing and wondered how she could sleep so soundly when he was finding it difficult to close his eyes.

He had come in late again from work like he had done so many times in the past. Before, his wife would stay awake and confront him whenever he came back, shouting at him for leaving her alone for hours. But today, she hadn't. He came back to find her sleeping in bed, not even flinching when he slid into bed with her.

He wondered what that meant, was she tired of him? Was she cheating? He couldn't know. He looked at the time, it was 2:45 am. She was sleeping so soundly, maybe it was because she had slipped out and gotten fucked to completion before he came in. He shook those thoughts out of his mind, it had been fifteen years and she hadn't cheated before, why would she start now?

He turned over to face his wife, taking in her blonde hair and curvy frame, and leaned over, sniffing her hair slightly. He didn't smell anyone else on her but what he did smell was that lavender perfume he loved so much. He felt his dick throb and he got the intense desire to lean over and kiss her neck.

He did just that, giving her soft kisses on the neck to wake her up. She roused slightly but stayed asleep, making Mike feel a little frustrated. He could feel his dick getting harder and he wanted his wife, he wanted her now.

He came closer to her and kissed her neck then sucked on it, hard enough to leave a mark. He moved his hand under the covers and slipped his hand underneath her pajama shirt, cupped her boob and squeezed lightly.

She let out a small moan, causing Mike to smirk lightly against her neck. She slapped his hand away and moved away from him. "Not now, Mike. I'm tired." She said softly.

Mike chuckled then kissed behind her ears. "C'mon, Sam." He moaned softly against her ear. "It's been weeks."

"It's been weeks because of you." She said, sitting up, fully awake now.

Mike could feel his boner going down and sighed. Well, he had no one to blame but himself, he had woken up the sleeping bear after all.

"Please don't start. It's 3 in the morning."

"And I'm sure you came in here at midnight from God-knows-where, doing God-knows-what with God-knows-who!" Sam said, facing her husband. She had waited up for him till midnight then decided it was no longer worth it and went to bed. Now he woke her up to have sex? Where did he get the nerve to do that?

"I was working, you know this!"

"Till midnight?" She scoffed at him, rolling her eyes. Oldest excuse in the book.

"Yes till midnight, it's not my fault that I've had to make more deliveries these past few weeks and besides the overtime gives me better pay, don't you want that?"

"What I want is my husband besides me during the dark hours of the day. What I want is a warm body to hold on to at night. What I want is someone to make me feel good." She said, her voice getting louder with each sentence.

"I can do that," he said, moving closer to her, "I can make you feel good."

He leaned closer and pressed a kiss to her lips softly at first and then harder. Sam gave in at first but then moved away. "Mike..." she started but he pressed his lips to hers again before she could contest once again.

Sam sighed and leaned into the kiss. Mike could feel his boner rising again and he slipped his hands underneath her shirt like he did earlier. This time she didn't contest it, instead she leaned back into the bed and let Mike do what he wanted.

Mike was excited and he moved quickly, taking off her shirt and then his. He cupped her breasts in his hands, alternating between light and hard squeezes. He brought his lips down from her lips to her nipple and took the left one in his mouth while his fingers played with the one on the right. He couldn't remember the last time he had her tits in her mouth and he wanted to take full advantage.

His tongue circled her nipple, earning light sighs from his wife. He sucked on it with vigor, his excitement only increasing. Sam wrapped her hands around her husband, getting into the swing of things. She arched her back, giving Mike more access to what he wanted.

The rest of their clothes melted away and Mike hurriedly searched through his wallet for a condom. He only had a small window of time before he completely lost his boner so he needed to find it fast. Sam rolled her eyes and grabbed him by his dick, bringing it close to her entrance.

"Forget the condom, we're no teenagers." She said, her voice seductive. Mike couldn't remember when his wife was so brazen and it wasn't like he didn't like it anyway. He reared his hips back and with a thrust, buried himself into his wife.

He groaned, feeling her pulsate around him. He thrusted into her quickly, propped up on his arms and gazing down at her heaving breasts. Sam's eyes were closed; she was concentrating, tightening the walls of her vagina so she could reach climax quickly with what little pleasure she was getting out of this.

Mike was having the time of his life, thrusting faster and faster. He placed his full body weight on Sam, who wrapped her legs around him. This created a tighter sensation around Mike that made Mike lose control. With a long groan and one last mighty thrust, he emptied himself into his wife.

He lay on top of her for a couple of seconds, still reeling from the intensity of his orgasm. He let out a breath then propped himself up on his hands, gazing down at the aftermath of what just happened. Sam had cum leaking out of her and her entire vulva was red.

"I'm sorry," Mike started, "I couldn't control it."

"It's fine. Anything up there waiting to be fertilized is way past its sell by date." Sam joked, throwing her legs off the edge of the bed and getting up.

Mike smiled. "Well that makes me feel a little better but I actually meant…"

"Don't worry about it, Mike. You know it takes me longer these days." Sam said good-naturedly, searching the bedside drawer for her vibrator. It didn't take her long to get there, in fact she could cum very quickly if she put her mind to it. But what good would it do if she made her husband feel guilty for not satisfying her? It was much easier to just finish up in the bathroom.

She grabbed the vibrator out of her nightstand, making sure to keep it out of Mike's sight. "I'm going to go clean up in the bathroom." she announced, walking away quickly so Mike wouldn't suspect anything.

When she closed the bathroom door behind her, Mike could hear the faint steady rhythm of vibration coming from it. He sighed and turned over in bed. He appreciated his wife for not making him feel guilty about it but it was a little emasculating to hear evidence of a toy bringing her to completion in a way that he couldn't.

After a few minutes, he heard a soft cry come from the bathroom signifying that his wife had reached orgasm. He waited for a few seconds then heard the classic flush meant to disguise what she had just spent the last few minutes doing in there.

When Sam came out and saw her husband had his back to the bathroom door, she breathed a sigh of relief, it would be easier this way to hide the vibrator. She walked over to her side of the bed, hid the vibrator in the drawer of the nightstand that had a lock, placed her phone on the top of the nightstand and closed her eyes, ready to drift off to sleep.

She found slumber that night but Mike couldn't sleep, haunted by the faint sound of her vibrator and the humiliating fact that he could not satisfy his wife.

CHAPTER TWO:
Endless Worries

Mike woke up the next morning and went to work with the sound and guilt still eating at him. He was on the road, at the helm of the delivery truck, trying to get some packages to a warehouse and all he could think about was his sex life in his marriage.

Last night was the first time in weeks that he had sex with his wife. He was attracted to her, he loved her but sometimes it felt like he was having sex with someone who was barely there. Last night just seemed to drive that statement in, she seemed into it at first but not enough to orgasm? He felt like something was lacking and if he could feel it then she probably felt it too.

But she hadn't said anything yet so perhaps he was only overthinking things. Just because his performance had been a little lack-luster last night didn't mean he couldn't get better or that their sex life was crumbling.

He shook his head and resolved to stop thinking about it. Instead of spending his time injecting negativity into his marriage, he could work on it. And that would involve getting back on time for once and trying to satisfy his wife as best he could tonight.

When he got back into the house later that night, he found his wife sleeping in bed. He glanced at his watch, 10:45 pm. Well that got rid of any ides of her cheating on him, she really did spend her nights waiting up for him which made him feel even more guilty.

He watched her sleep, taking in the beauty that was his wife. Even at 43, she was still the most beautiful woman he had ever met and he loved her just as much as he did as a 30 year old man when he married her 15 years ago.

It bothered him to think that something might be wrong with them, with him. It was getting harder to, well, stay hard and he couldn't last as long as he did when he was younger but he tried didn't he, to please her? He always gave it his best shot but it seemed his best was no longer cutting it.

His eyes fell on Sam's phone resting on the nightstand and he grew curious. She had it on her when she went to the bathroom last night, probably using it to watch or read something smutty. If he went through it, it would give him an idea of what she liked. Understanding her desires would help him fulfill them after all.

Not thinking beyond that, he took her phone off the nightstand and debated whether or not to unlock it. He had her passcode but she hadn't given it to him so he could snoop. With a deep sigh, and shutting down the guilt he felt in his chest, he entered her passcode and began scrolling through her phone.

He didn't find anything in her search history which made sense. If she was searching for something inappropriate, she wouldn't leave the evidence lying around. He decided to navigate to her social media instead, there were all those porn pages online, maybe she went there to look for something to watch.

His search landed him in a forum that he did not expect, "BBC fantasies." His pulse quickened and he tapped the thread.

The screen filled with images of big, tall black men railing older white women. He watched as video upon video of white women cheating on their partners with "BBC" came onto the page. He felt even more inadequate but strangely aroused when he watched a video of a black man fucking the shit out of someone's wife while he watched in the corner. There were stories of women escaping in the night while their husbands or boyfriends were asleep, seeking big black cocks that could satisfy them in a way that their partners could not.

It looked like Sam had been on this thread for months, watching these videos and reading these stories. Was this what she wanted? Is this what it took for her to cum nowadays, this and a vibrator apparently. A chill went through him, was she cheating on him after all?

Mike set the phone down, his mind racing. He could feel jealousy rising in him but there was another feeling as well. He looked down and sure enough, he was sporting a boner. Even if he felt inadequate he had to admit, the idea that Sam had been with someone else made him excited, but why?

This was clearly something she craved, something she wanted but what if she had already gotten it? What would he do if he found out that she hadn't been loyal to him?

Sam stirred in bed and opened her eyes slowly. She sat up in surprise. "You're home?" She quickly glanced at her bedside clock. "It's only 11pm."

"I know. I wanted to surprise you." He said, smiling.

Sam was confused but happy to see that her husband was in the house at this time for once. "Do you want to come to bed?"

Mike wasn't sure. He did have a boner he would like to take care of but he had so many conflicting feelings.

"We need to talk about something first."

Sam's brows furrowed in concern but Mike attempted to reassure her with a smile. "Is everything okay? Oh my goodness, were you fired? Is that why you're home?"

"I found the threads Sam."

Sam looked at him with confusion in her eyes but then recognition came into them. "Oh my goodness." She said, burying her face in her hands.

"Look Mike, I know you have a lot of questions…"

Mike raised his hand to cut her off. "I just have one honestly, are you cheating on me?"

Sam opened her eyes wide. "No no no! Of course not, I would never. I love you."

Mike looked into her eyes and in that moment, he believed her. He felt reassured now which brought him to his next question.

"When did this start? Is this something you want to do?"

"I don't know." She said, lifting her face out of her hands. "I honestly don't know. The whole thing was harmless at first, I was searching online for some porn to get me off and then I found this one video that made me feel…things."

"Things you don't feel with me?" Mike asked. That came out harsher than he wanted it to but he had to know.

Sam didn't say anything for some time and then she sighed. "Mike, I love you but you know that things haven't been the best...in that area. You're never home and when you are, we barely have sex. When we do have sex, I have to finish off in the bathroom because..."

"Because I don't make you cum? Is that it?"

"I think it's more than that if I'm being honest. We never try anything new, I mean it's been 15 years and we haven't even tried out a new position. I've seen women who look like me getting bent in ways that I didn't even know were possible and I have to admit, the thought of being those women, of being fucked by some of those men...well, it gets me there."

"I think I understand that but I don't know. Do you want to do that?" Mike asked, looking at his wife and studying her reaction.

"I would never cheat on you." Sam said, resolutely.

"Yeah but I can't expect you to keep running off to the bathroom to finish up every time we have sex. It's emasculating. I get all the satisfaction I could want from you."

Sam scoffed.

"What's that for?"

"You know that's not true. You're a man so it's easy for you to get there but I know that you know our sex life isn't the best. You're telling me that I'm always what you think about when you're getting off by yourself?"

Mike couldn't say anything but he knew she was right. They were spending less and less time together and even when they were, he wasn't exactly thinking about her if he wanted to climax. But somehow this was different, some of those threads featured people who actively wanted to step out of their marriages and that wasn't something that he wanted to do.

But then he thought about the ones he saw where the husband sat and watched his wife doing it with another man and he felt the boner start to rise again. Maybe that was something he wanted to do.

"If you had the chance to do this, have sex with a bbc, would you take it?" He asked her.

"Not if it upset you." Sam responded.

"What if it didn't? And what if I wanted to watch?"

Sam moved closer to her husband and held his hand. "What are you saying"

"I'm saying, I want us to do this. Let's find someone and make this fantasy a reality."

CHAPTER THREE:
Unveiling Fantasies

"Are you sure about this?" Sam asked, the doubt creeping into her voice. She had gotten excited when Mike proposed the both of them working through this fantasy together but now she wasn't sure.

"Wouldn't it be less extreme to just search new positions online and try them out?" She asked.

Mike was already super into this idea and he knew that his wife was too but he didn't need her backing out now. He needed her to stay on board this train.

He squeezed her hand reassuringly. "Yes I am and you are too. We are doing this together."

A laptop hummed between them, the screen displaying a popular dating site for people looking for big black cocks. The both of them felt nervous but excited at the same time.

"How did you even find this place anyway?" Sam asked.

"I just had to search it up and I've seen reviews on it, it seems decent."

"*Looking to date, romance or have sex with a hot, young black stud well this is where to meet them! These handsome young singles are looking to satisfy you in every way you want.*" the site read.

They went through the sign-up process together, they could sign up for a joint profile so they did. Sam selected a decent photo of the two of them and they crafted out their bio to show what they were looking for.

"Adventurous, loving couple looking for a respectful and confident young man to join us. Must be understanding, respectful of boundaries and ready to explore new things. Discretion is a must." their profile read.

"That looks okay, doesn't it?" Sam asked, looking to her husband for approval.

He nodded. "That's right. Now all we need to do is wait for people to sign up and then we can go through them together and talk to the ones we like."

"What does this mean for you though? Is this like a threesome kind of thing?" Sam asked. She knew what she wanted but what did her husband want out of the whole thing?

"Threesome? Oh no, I'm fine with watching, excited by the thought of it actually." Mike said. "Let's just talk to the guys and we'll move from there okay?"

Within hours of creating their profile, messages began flooding in. Over the next few days, Sam would sift through all the responses while Mike was at work and when he came back, they would check through the profiles together. Some of the messages were polite, other ones were explicit with the men just sending pictures of their junk and others were downright strange, describing all the weird things they wanted to do with both Mike and Sam.

The ones they liked, they set up video calls with. The first guy was a polite young man in his mid-twenties but he couldn't stop talking about himself. Sam thought that someone who was that self-involved wouldn't be much of a giver in the bedroom.

The second guy that they interviewed was a handsome man that seemed perfect at first but then all of a sudden he started listing out all of the demands he wanted from Sam. The both of them grew uncomfortable and ended the call quickly not wanting to get involved with someone like that.

The third guy was very attractive but he was overly flirtatious and seemed more interested in the idea of hooking up with Mike than Sam and this was more for her than him.

After more interviews like that, they began to feel disheartened. That was until they connected with Jay.

Jay seemed perfect and stood out as soon as they connected with him over the computer. He was a well-spoken man, confident and very respectful, putting them at ease almost immediately. He was in his early thirties and gave off a natural charisma that immediately drew them in.

"Hi Jay," Sam started, sounding instantly relieved by how charismatic this man seemed. "It's really lovely to meet you."

"Nice to meet you too." He replied with a warm smile. "I'm happy the both of you set this up, I was hoping to get to know your expectations before we got into anything?"

Sam and Mike looked at each other, pretty sure that they had just found their guy. As they kept talking, it became clear that Jay was everything they were looking for. He wasn't crass, he seemed interested in their desires and asked thoughtful questions. He didn't feel like someone storming into their marriage, he felt like he wanted to be a willing participant.

"We are loving this but do you mind if we set up a meeting in real life. We just want to see how this energy comes off in person." Mike asked.

Jay smiled warmly. "Of course. Just name the time and the place, I'll be there."

They set up a meeting with Jay at a nearby bar. Mike and Sam were pleased to find out they weren't being catfished when Jay came walking through the bar doors. They were a little worried that maybe the computer had warped his face or something but no, he looked just as handsome as he did on that video call.

Jay was a striking man, 6 foot 2, muscular, broad shoulders and smooth dark skin. He had short-cropped hair, a neat trimmed beard and Mike and Sam watched as his brown eyes searched for them in the crowd. He was wearing a tight, snug white shirt and his smile was inviting.

He found them sitting by the bar and walked over to them. He flashed a smile at Sam. "You look stunning." He said, giving her a lingering look.

"You don't look too bad yourself." She responded.

"It's nice to meet you two in person. You seem different from most people you find on sites like that." He said, shaking Mike's hand and giving Sam a polite hug.

"Different? In what way?" Mike asked.

"Like you're looking for something more, some people would have asked for a dick pic but you set up interviews."

"We love each other and things had been lacking so my husband decided he would let me go out there and experience one of my greatest fantasies…"

"A BBC? Classic." Jay said, chuckling slightly.

"We don't mean anything by it…" Mike interjected, hoping they weren't being offensive in some way.

"You're good, I find it flattering. And I have to admit, I'd be honored if you ended up choosing me."

"Oh we're well on our way there, we just need to know what you're all about." Sam asked.

"What do you mean?"

"Well you seem a little too good to be true. Why is a guy like you on a site like that?"

Jay chuckled then raised his hands to signal to the bartender. "Three beers please." He said before turning to the couple once again.

"I'm a man with very specific skills," He said, his voice velvety, leaning closer to the both of them, "and I like to use those skills on people who are very deserving."

Sam could feel heat start to spread all over her body, pooling between her legs. Something about this man was drawing her in and her mind was already full of dirty thoughts involving him bending her over and driving into her over and over.

Their beers came and Jay reached out to take a sip out the glass. Sam watched the foam from the beer stick to his mustache and the way he used his tongue to wipe it away. The heat between her legs turned into throbbing and she couldn't wait for them to skip this whole interview and get right to business.

"So tell me what are your boundaries?" Jay asked.

Sam glanced at Mike, who nodded in encouragement. "We just want to make sure everything is consensual and there's lots of communication involved. Mike will be present and...involved." She said the last word with as much innuendo she could muster.

"So he'll watch?" Jay asked, raising an eyebrow.

Mike nodded. "We want to make sure there's mutual respect and understanding in all of this."

"Of course, those are my top priorities as well. I'm sure this can be a positive experience for all of us. So are we doing this?"

Sam looked at Mike and he looked right back at her. They knew the answer to that, they had found their guy. They nodded at Jay together, who clapped.

"Great. So let's pound back a couple of beers and get this started shall we?"

CHAPTER FOUR:
Surrounding Control

A couple of beers later, Mike had to go use the bathroom and that was when Jay made his move. He studied her face then came closer to her, leaning over till his mouth practically grazed her lips.

"You seem so wound up, a couple minutes with me and I bet I could make you come...loose." He said in a low voice that gave her butterflies. He leaned back and looked directly into her eyes, waiting for her reaction.

Sam swallowed and looked away, unable to meet his gaze. The moment suddenly felt charged and she knew what she wanted now, she wanted this man to take her.

She grabbed her beer and pounded it back, needing it to loosen her tongue. When she felt the rush from the alcohol passing through her, she looked at him and whispered, "What's it going to take to get a few minutes with you?"

He chuckled, loving her newfound boldness. "I don't need anything from you little miss, just your body. I have a hotel room not too far from here. If you and your husband are interested, we could go over there and I could...ravish you."

Mike appeared from the bathroom and saw his wife getting close with this man. He was supposed to be feeling jealous but instead all he could feel was excitement, excitement that only grew when Sam suggested going to Jay's hotel room.

He hadn't expected that things would go this fast and while they were on their way there in Jay's car, he still could hardly believe it but it all became real when they walked into his room and he shut the door behind them.

"The both of you are okay with anything that happens in this room?" Jay asked, moving closer to Sam as he said this.

Sam and Mike nodded in unison and Jay made his move. He took Sam into his arms and pressed a kiss to her lips. At first it was soft, getting her comfortable, teasing her before fully claiming it like it was his from the start.

Sam meets his kiss with a surprising hunger, desperate to quench that fire that had built between her legs. All Mike could do was watch from the corner as another man, a bigger man, a darker man, ran his hands all over his wife. He should feel jealous, tear him off her but all he felt was a raging boner growing in his pants at the sight.

Jay pulled away from Sam, his eyes glassy, aroused. Sam was an attractive woman, that was one of the things he noticed about her when he saw their joint profile. Blonde, blue eyes, shapely with wide hips and a lovely set of breasts. He didn't know what was going on with her and her husband but he was determined to show that body all the love it needed.

Jay couldn't hold himself out and grabbed her again, pushing her up against the wall and grinding his erection against her. His hands stroked her skin, his lips found her neck and he sucked at it intensely, earning a soft moan from Sam. He heard movement from the corner Mike was in and out of the corner of his eye, saw him take out his phone.

Good, let him record so he could learn just the right way to treat a woman like this.

"I need to fuck you." Jay frowned against her neck. Sam was taken aback by such language. It was so vulgar, so laden with desire. When was the last time someone had made her feel this wanted, when was the last time someone had made it so clear that they needed her body.

Sam could smell the beer on his breath as he claimed her lips once again, that coupled with his touch made for a heady combination that intoxicated her. His left hand cupped her face while the right undid all the buttons on her shirt, revealing her white bra that could be unclasped from the front. He did that, letting her breasts out of their lacy cage.

A finger grazed her nipple lightly then his mouth followed shortly after. Sam threw her head back as she felt the heat and wetness from his mouth on her nipples. His tongue swirled her nipple and he sucked on it, sending pleasure radiating through Sam.

She rubbed herself against him, the fire down there rising even more. Taking the cue, he slipped his hands into the waistband of her jeans, his mouth still working wonders on her nipples. His hands head directly for her clit and he strokes it lightly. Sam could feel an orgasm start to build and she was so ready to let go, this would be the first time she came without a vibrator.

Jay slipped a finger into Sam, smirking against her nipple slightly. She let out a moan, feeling the pressure building in her. He moved his finger faster and faster while she bucked her hips against them, causing more pleasure to build until Sam felt she would come undone.

"Cum for me, you can do it." He whispered into her ears, moving his fingers within her faster. Sam's breathing got louder until she felt herself let go, cumming all over his fingers. Her knees get weak and Jay has to hold her up with his strength. She hadn't felt that much pleasure in such a long time and she felt on top of the world.

"I'm not done with you yet." Jay said, smiling at her. He looked in Mike's direction who was sporting a boner. "You still recording?" He asked.

Mike put the phone down. "I'm sorry, I just couldn't resist."

"You're good, keep recording. I want you to go back and see exactly how to please your wife."

"I'm not done with you yet." He said, pushing Sam towards the bed. He took off the rest of her clothes then his shirt and out of the pocket of his jeans, he took out a small square.

He took off his jeans, then his boxers and his dick springs up in front of Sam who can only look at it in awe.

"I-I don't think that will fit." She said, genuinely worried.

"You'll be fine, trust me" He walked over and leaned over. Feeling emboldened, Sam grabbed his length causing him to gasp. She stroked him and he closed. his eyes, letting himself embrace the pleasure.

He brought the condom packet he had taken out of his pocket and tore it open, slipping it on. He climbed on top of her then claimed her mouth once again. He pulled her legs apart and then positioned his dick in her entrance.

"If it gets overwhelming then just let me know." He said, before sliding into her slowly, closing his eyes in pleasure.

Mike watched as Jay climbed on top of his wife, getting ready to penetrate her. He could see the expression on her face, she was excited to receive him, excited to have him in her. A part of him had felt jealous when he watched Jay make his wife orgasm, something he hadn't been able to do in a long time but he couldn't ignore the other feeling; the one of anticipation. He wanted his wife to get fucked by this man.

Seeing Sam so eager to receive a dick that was much bigger than his made him feel a kind of excitement that he hadn't felt before. He got his phone ready and took a seat on a chair nearby, he was going to record everything that happened today.

CHAPTER FIVE: Coital Bliss

The phone's camera in Mike's zoomed in on the place where Jay and Sam were connected. Jay was asking slow, gentle thrusts into Sam to get her used to him while Mike worked the camera, struggling with how much the sight turned him on.

He couldn't take it any longer, he had to touch himself. He passed the camera into his non-dominant hand while he unzipped his pants with his dominant one. He took out his dick, only half the size of Jay's and started stroking it to the sounds Sam was making whilst under Jay, to the sound of his skin slapping against hers.

He imagines it was him for a second, making his wife make those loud moans but that thought didn't turn him on half as much as watching Jay and Sam did. Sam was holding onto him for dear life whilst Jay went in and out of her in a steady, firm rhythm. How could Sam handle all of that?

"You like that?" Jay sighed into Sam's ear. Sam loved it, every thrust into her felt like a thousand stars were exploding in parts of her she didn't even know existed. She grabbed his waist, not wanting him to stop and pulled him deeper into her, she wanted him to fill her completely.

Jay groaned and sank into her, increasing the force of his thrusts. If this woman wanted more of him, he would give her more. "Fuck," he murmured against her neck, feeling himself getting closer and closer. He hadn't expected her to feel this good, he couldn't believe a pussy this good had wasted on that man for years. That didn't matter now though, because he was going to show it and her all the love it deserved.

He went faster, causing Sam to cry out. He leaned over and whispered into her ear, "Come for me, you can do it. Fuck, you feel so fucking good." He punctuated each word with a thrust, letting the sensation run through him. "I'm so close." He groaned.

Sam couldn't believe that she was making such a man feel these things, did she really drive this man that crazy? Was this all just part of the experience he was used to providing or was this something more. She couldn't figure it out, all she knew in that moment was this man wanted her and couldn't get enough of her. He was driving himself into her, over and over again because he needed her and that was enough to make her come undone.

She let out a long, drawn out sigh as wave after wave of pleasure washed over her. Nothing had made her feel like this before, not her husband, not even her vibrator. She buckled and shook underneath Jay holding unto him for dear life while he went to town on her, free to pound away into her as hard as he could now that he had gotten her to come.

"Fuck, fuck, uhhhh." He groaned, the muscles in his arms growing taut. Sam could feel his dick pulsating in her as he came. In the corner, Mike was stroking his dick furiously, incredibly aroused by everything he had just seen, he had no idea his wife was capable of making such sounds. He came into his hands, his own groan washed out by the sounds Jay was making.

He looked down at the mess he had made, cum all over his hands and his pants. He looked up at Jay who had taken his wife's lips once again, he saw the way Sam held on to Jay like he was her lifeline and he felt his dick twitch to life once again, this was an incredibly hot scene.

Jay stood up and went to the bathroom, coming back with some wipes for Sam. He took the time to clean her up before heading back to clean himself up as well. When he came back, he found Mike on the bed beside his wife, red in the face from stroking himself. Sam was back in her clothes, her hair tousled from their encounter, looking the picture of post-coital bliss.

"So," he started, taking his pants off the ground and putting them back on. "How would you rate your first BBC experience?" He threw this question at Sam whose eyes lit up immediately.

"Ten out of ten!" She exclaimed. "I didn't even know I could-"

"Scream like a banshee in bed?" Jay said, chuckling. "I told you all I needed was a couple of minutes with you. And you, Mike? How do you feel?"

"I feel...surprisingly good. I think you may have taught this old dog some new tricks even." He said, smiling widely. He reached out and took his wife's hand who squeezed it.

"Thank you for being open to this, Mike." Sam said, placing a chaste kiss on her husband's forehead. "I don't know a lot of men who would be okay with their wives..." she trailed off, as her mind went back to all the dirty things that Jay had done to her.

Jay chuckled to himself. He had to admit, in all his years of providing these kinds of services to disgruntled white couples, this was the most unique one he had ever encountered. And Sam? She didn't see like a woman who wanted to stick it to her husband, she looked like someone who had a lot of love to give and that made Jay intrigued.

He dug into the pockets of his pants and brought out his card. "If you ever need me or my services, or if you're ever in the mood for a beer and a good conversation, call me." He said, handing the card over to Mike and Sam.

"So does this mean that we'll see you again?" Sam asked, as she and Mike stood up to head to the door.

"Of course you'll see me again." Jay said, grabbing Sam and kissing her deeply once again. He smacked her ass as she walked away, causing her to get red in the face. "No way I'm letting a nice piece of ass like this go to waste."

Sam and Mike made their way back to the bar where they met Jay, their car still in the parking lot. When they got home, all they could think about was what happened at Jay's hotel room.

"How much did you record?" Sam asked.

"Everything." Mike said, taking out his phone and showing her the footage. Sam could feel throbbing down there all over again as she visually relived all of the things that Jay had done to her back at the hotel.

"Seeing everything from that perspective. It's all so...dirty." Sam said. "Did I ever sound like that when I was with you?"

"Not even close." Mike said, laughing even though he really should feel jealous. "I think the last time I heard your scream like that was maybe when we first got married."

Sam chuckled. "Yeah, you definitely knew a few tricks back then." The smile from her face fell. "Is it bad that I want to do it again? Feel those things again?"

Mike shook his head. "Is it bad that I want to watch you do it again?"

"No it's not but it's just...what if I become addicted to it or something? What if I don't want to stop or the only thing that can make me cum is a big black cock?"

"Well then," Mike started. "I better start getting used to seeing more of Jay around."

CHAPTER SIX: A New Identity

Sam found herself alone in her living room, her fingers hovering over the keyboard of the laptop in front of her. It was a weekday so of course, Mike had left her all alone to go to work. On other days, she would lament her lack of employment but not today. Today, she was lurking on a hot wives community forum, reading up on stories similar to hers.

She had known that there was a name for women like her, women who were open to being sexual with other men outside of their husbands and like her husband, some of the partners of these women liked to watch the sexual encounters as well. Sam wasn't sure if she wanted to sleep with other men outside of Jay but she did know that after her first session with him, she was excited by the idea.

She took a deep breath, she had been wondering if she could share her story. She felt like she needed to talk about this with someone other than her husband and she didn't have any other girlfriends so this was the only other option. Her fingers hesitated over the keyboard then she started typing, recounting her night with Jay and everything that came with it.

"A couple of days ago, I had my first experience with a black bull. For context, I'm a 43 year old white woman who has been married for 15 years. I love my husband but things have been a bit dull in the sack lately. I had been lurking on some forums like this and my husband found out then let me have sex

outside our marriage on the condition that he watched.

It was the most incredible, intense and most liberating time of my life. He absolutely dominated me and made me feel things that I have never felt before. My husband is fully supportive and I even feel more connected to him but I don't know what this means for us now. Is this a one time thing because I don't want it to be, I like the idea of getting railed by a big dick but I don't know how long my husband can be comfortable with it. Anyway, I just wanted to share my story."

Sam hit "post" then watched as the words that she wrote went live on the forum. She wasn't sure how long it would take for people to respond but she was surprised to find the notifications pouring in almost immediately. She clicked through the first replies, all of them supportive.

"I just had my first bull too, best time of my life!"

"My husband loves to watch me get railed by a thick bull too, love that for you!"

"It sounds like you had an amazing experience. Don't stop exploring."

"You know what they say! 'When you go black, you can't go back!'"

There was one that really stood out to her though. One that seemed to understand the confusion that she was feeling right now.

"Hi there! I was in a similar position a while back as well, married long term but lacking in the bedroom. I tried everything to bring the spice back, not just in our sex life but in our love life as well until I decided to take matters into my own hands and fuck someone more endowed than my husband. I didn't care if my husband was involved or not, I had tried to heighten our sex life but it wasn't taking so I decided to be a

little selfish. Eventually though, he started watching and we've never been happier. My advice would be to not overthink this, think about your own satisfaction. You're not too old to enjoy sex and if you've found a way to have it in a more fulfilling way then go for it. Take the bull by the horns girl!"

This anonymous commenter filled her heart with warmth. She had read through every single comment, soaking in the encouragement from the community but this particular one spoke to her. How many times had she tried to awaken the spark in her life with Mike? She loved her husband but things had been so mundane for a long time. She had finally found something to make her feel good, in a way that she deserved so she was going to embrace it. Mike would just have to get on board.

Motivated by the supportive comments from the rest of the hot wives community she decided to have a conversation with her husband when she came back home.

When Mike came back, Sam was ready to be completely honest. She wanted the both of them to have an open conversation about Jay and how this would affect them moving forward.

Mike walked into their bedroom and kissed Sam on her cheek. "Hey honey, I hope you weren't too lonely at home today?"

Sam watched as her husband took off his work clothes and took in his body. He was no stud like Jay but he had his charm. She had no intention of leaving their marriage but maybe there was a version of their marriage that had Jay in it and any other man she would be interested in.

"I actually wasn't lonely, I spent most of the day online reading up on other women like me."

"Other women like you?" Mike asked, raising an eyebrow. What was this about?

"Other women who have been with men outside their marriage. I posted about our experience on the 'hot wives' forum and I got a lot of support. It also made me realize something."

Mike said felt anxiety wash over him. What was she trying to say? Was Sam trying to tell him that she was no longer interested in their relationship? He had thought this whole thing with Jay may have been a one time thing like having a threesome when your relationship got too boring but what if it made her realize that she could do so much better than him.

"Please don't leave me." He blurted out.

"What?!" Sam exclaimed. "What do you mean? I don't want to leave you!"

Mike blinked in surprise. "You don't?"

"Of course not, I love you."

"But things have been so lackluster lately." Mike said. What was he saying? His wife had just told him that she wanted to stay so why was he looking for excuses for her?

"Of course they have been, we've been married for 15 years, things would get a little monotonous but what I realized wasn't that I want to leave you."

"So what did you realize?" Mike asked.

"I realized that I don't want to stop this thing we've started. I really enjoyed that first time with Jay and I want to do it again and maybe not even just with Jay, maybe with other men as well." She said, reaching for his hand and squeezing it.

Mike raised his eyebrows slightly but he didn't pull away. "You want to sleep with other men?"

"Yes," Sam admitted, her voice not even shaking. "It's really exciting and I want to take charge of my sex life in this way, it's fulfilling in a way that I didn't expect. I think this is something that I need to do for myself and I want to know if you would be okay with that."

Mike went silent for some time, trying to process her words. She didn't want to leave him but she did want to step out of their marriage. How did he feel about that? He knew how he was supposed to feel;

angry, jealous and maybe even a little disgusted by the proposal but then he thought back to the time he watched Jay fuck his wife, how aroused he was by the fact and he knew what he wanted to say.

"Sam, I have to admit, it was a little strange watching you sleep with Jay but then it really turned me on. I loved watching you experience that much pleasure, it made me happy seeing you so fulfilled."

"Wait, so you're not upset or jealous?"

Mike shook his head. "No, I'm not. It's unconventional but I can definitely see you doing that again, I only hope you can let me watch it every now and again. I don't think I've ever come as much as I did that day."

"Oh! Thank you, thank you, thank you! Your support means everything to me." She said, bringing her husband close and hugging him tight.

He smiled, hugging her back. "I trust you Sam and if you want to explore this further, you have my full support and permission."

"I do want that and I was hoping you'd let me invite Jay over when you're out working tomorrow?" She said, her voice hopeful that he would agree.

"Of course, I just need you to do one favor."

"And what's that?" Sam asked, curious.

"Record it for me. I want to watch it later."

CHAPTER SEVEN:
Mingling Desires

Sam was feeling good after her conversation with her husband the other day but it still took her some time before she felt brave enough to reach out to Jay. She felt a burning desire to see him again and have him explore her body all over again but she hesitated every time she reached for her phone to call the number on his card.

It wasn't until a week later that she finally swallowed all her anxiety and reached for her phone to text him, her fingers no longer trembling as they typed out the text.

"I've been thinking about our time together and I would love to see you again." - Sam.

A response came almost immediately.

"I haven't been able to get you out of my mind. I'm glad you reached out, meet me at the bar we first hung out in an hour." – Jay

Sam arrived first. She chose a corner table, one that was away from prying eyes and sat down to order, ordered a beer then waited in with bated breath and anticipation. Her drink came and she sipped it nervously, checking her phone for any sort of communication from Jay.

Finally, she saw him walk in, his presence commanding. Jay spotted her and smiled then waved, making his way over to her. Her pulse quickened as he walked over to her and took a seat across from her.

"Hey," Jay said, smiling at her. His voice was smoother and deep, and it brought back memories of when he was whispering sexy things into her ear while he was deep within her.

"Hi, Jay," she said, her voice coming out breathless and choked. "I have been looking forward to this. I've actually been really nervous leading up to this, I'm surprised you wanted to meet up at all." She was rambling and she hoped that didn't turn Jay off.

"Hey," he said, reaching out and taking her hands in his. He locked his eyes onto hers and she felt such a magnetic pull to him in that moment. "Don't overthink this, I had fun with you and I want to keep having fun with you. You look amazing by the way."

She smiled and tucked her a strand behind her ears, blushing. "Thank you, so do you."

They started chatting, Jay leaning in, his eyes never leaving hers. He seemed to be gazing right into her soul and it made her feel like she was the only person in the room.

"Do you mind if I ask you something?" She asked, suddenly.

"Sure you can, go ahead."

"Please don't take offense to this but you seem so put together. I just mean that out of all the guys that my husband and I saw on that site, you are the least sleazy. What made you sign up on a place like that?"

Jay chuckled and took a sip out of his beer that just arrived. "Everyone has their kinks and mine is making people's fantasies come true. I'm very particular about the kind of people I get involved with, you and your husband seemed genuine and I wanted to be involved in that."

"Besides," he said, his voice taking a more intimate tone, "It doesn't hurt that there's an attractive woman in the mix. It pains me to think that someone like you isn't getting all the fulfillment she needs. I want to fix that, I just need you to let me."

Sam felt heat rush to her cheeks, this man was very alluring. "And what if I want that, what if I want you to let you?"

"Then why don't we take this somewhere more private and I can show you all the wonders we can experience together."

Sam's breath hitched and her eyes widened. The way Jay was looking at her made her pulse quicken and that smile, that cocky smile, made her melt. "My husband isn't home, could we go to mine? My car's right outside."

Jay leaned back, his lips curling into a sexy smile and his eyes darkened with lust. "Lead the way, my lady."

The drive to her house was charged, she couldn't wait for what was coming. Her mind raced with thoughts of what was to come, her body hummed with excitement. She kept stealing glances at Jay, her hands gripping the wheel of the car tight as his hands roamed all over her thigh. Being around him was so intoxicating and she felt liberated in a way that she hadn't felt in a long time.

When they got to her house, Sam led her inside. She led him into her bedroom and sat on the bed while he towered over her. Jay stepped closer, cupping her cheek with his hand.

"Do you really want this?" he asked, his voice gentle and his eyes filled with desire.

Sam nodded, her eyes locking onto his. "Yes, I'm very sure."

Jay's lips curved into a sultry smile. "Then let's not waste any more time."

He leaned in to kiss her and she felt a rush of emotions run through her, the foremost of which was deep, burning desire.

"Oh wait, my husband asked me to record this for him. Is that okay? There's a camcorder in the bedside drawer and we can set it up."

"Yeah that's fine." He said, walking over to the drawer. He took out the camcorder and set it up on a shelf that stood opposite and in the direct sight of the bed. When he put it on, he walked over to her and pushed her into the bed.

"Let's get started then." He said, claiming her lips in a deep, passionate kiss.

Jay pushed a hand under her shirt and into her bra, freeing one breast. Like a flash, his mouth closed onto the nipple, sucking on it through the shirt. Sam felt a desire pool between her legs as his tongue made patterns all over. her sensitive nipples.

His hand slipped into her pants while another unzipped his pants. Sam was impatient so she tried to push his own pants down. Before she knew it, the both of them were naked and he was grinding his erection against her clit, making heR gasp in bliss.

He slipped his hard erection into her, and her eyes rolled back as her body embraced him. He hissed as he buried himself in her. "Yessss..." he groaned, his eyes glassy as he drove himself into her. He had only just entered her and he was already panting like he couldn't get enough of her or like he was close. Either way, it drove Sam to the brink of madness as she lay there in disbelief that she was bringing this man that much pleasure.

Feeling brazen, she rolled Jay off of her and got on top of her. She wanted him badly, so she straddled him. She could already imagine how his dick would feel when she slid down the length.

She raised her hips and took him inside of her, going down slowly, inch by him. His eyes rolled to the back of his head and he opened his mouth in a silent groan. She squeezed her muscle around him and slid down the rest of his length, taking him fully in.

She began to move up and down, Jay jerked his hips up to meet her, matching her thrust for thrust. It felt amazing and Sam could feel her own orgasm building in her. She couldn't remember the last time she had done this, it had been years. The last time she had ridden a man was during the early years of her marriage and now here she was, bouncing up and down another man's penis like she was a young cowgirl.

He gripped her hips and began to grind her against him. He tightened his jaw and let out a short, hoarse gasp as Sam went up and down and grinded her clit against him. She leaned forward and he took a nipple into his mouth. He rolled the nipple around in his mouth with his tongue, sucking on it like his life depended on it.

"I want you to bounce on this dick like you want to break it. Show that pretty pussy off to your husband, let him see how much you love taking this big dark cock in you, c'mon." He said, driving himself into her by bucking his hips.

Sam could feel the pressure building in her and she grinded down on him hard. That was all it took for her to come all over him. She let out a loud, long moan and collapsed on top of him, the muscle of her walls contracting all over Jay's dick.

Jay held on to her hips, pounding her as he sought his own release. He closed his eyes and his face contorted due to the ecstasy he was feeling. Sam could feel his dick pulsing in her as he gave one last, hard thrust and came in her. They weren't wearing a condom, and under normal circumstances she should be worried that another man was filling her with his seed but she couldn't care less. All she cared about was the way he throbbed in her, the sound of his groan and the way his hands gripped her hips tightly while he emptied himself into her.

He chuckled and raised her hips off slightly so her vagina was in full view of the camcorder. "I want your husband to see my cum dripping out of you." He said, as he watched his cum fall out of her and onto his body.

Sam laughed and rolled off him, letting herself come down from all the pleasure she had just experienced.

"That was..incredible." she said, sighing in post-coital bliss.

"Oh honey," he laughed, wrapping his arm around her and placing a soft kiss on her forehead. "That was only the beginning."

Jay looked at her intensely, so intensely it gave her butterflies. She was the farthest thing from a schoolgirl yet this man was able to make her feel like a teenager again.

"Why are you looking at me like that?" She asked him.

He hesitated, his eyes seemingly searching hers. He seemed to be weighing his next words carefully. "I think...I might want more."

Her eyes opened wide. "W-what does more mean?"

He sighed. "It means that I might be considering this arrangement. I don't know, I just get the sense that there's something here. Something more than just sex."

Sam sat up and used the sheets to cover herself. "You do realize I'm married right?"

"Yeah and you're fucking me? C'mon be for real, you wouldn't be with me if part of you wasn't over your husband."

Sam blinked rapidly, taken aback by his audacity. "I love my husband, I made that clear to you from the start."

"The both of you can say whatever makes you feel better about this but I've been here too many times and I know the truth. The sooner you accept it, the better. You and your husband may be on the last leg but we…we still have a shot."

Sam couldn't believe what she was hearing. She liked having sex with Jay, yes but that didn't give him the right to talk about her marriage in that way.

"I think you need to leave." She said, her tone firm.

Jay's eyebrows creased. "C'mon don't be like that." He said, reaching for her.

She dodged his touch and walked towards the door. "I told you at the beginning that you needed to respect my connection with my husband. I don't appreciate you insinuating I should leave him for you."

"So what? You're going to dump me?" Jay asked, looking a little sad by that prospect.

"I don't think this is going to work out, not if you're going to try to get in the way of me and my husband." Sam said.

Jay sighed and took his clothes off the floor, walking over to the door. He looked at her with a pained look in his eyes.

"You don't have to-"

Sam raised her hand to stop him from talking and he took the hint, walking away. When Sam was alone she walked over to her bed and buried her face in her hands.

Was this the last time she would ever see Jay?"

THE END

Dear reader,

Thank you for reading to the end! I hope the book lived up to your expectations!

Would you like to read part two? It's available at Amazon as well; just go to this book's product page or series page!

Exclusive erotic short story club
Want even more? You can join my exclusive erotic short club **for free**. By doing so, you will get a bunch of free stories (before I publish

them on Amazon), audiobook coupon codes, and much more! Join here: https://bit.ly/3WJsqRp

Or email me at amber.carden.books@gmail.com and I will send you a link!

Amber

© Copyright 2024 - All rights reserved.

The content contained within this book may not be reproduced, duplicated, or transmitted without direct written permission from the author or the publisher.

This book is copyright protected. It is only for personal use. You cannot amend, distribute, sell, use, quote or paraphrase any part, or the content within this book, without the consent of the author or publisher.

www.ingramcontent.com/pod-product-compliance
Lightning Source LLC
LaVergne TN
LVHW041627070526
838199LV00052B/3272